# THE BREMEN TOWN GHOSTS

by Wiley Blevins • illustrated by Steve Cox

RED CHAIR
• PRESS •

Please visit our website at **www.redchairpress.com** for more high-quality products for young readers.

## About the Author

**Wiley Blevins** has taught elementary school in both the United States and South America. He has also written over 70 books for children and 15 for teachers, as well as created reading programs for schools in the U.S. and Asia with Scholastic, Macmillan/McGraw-Hill, Houghton Mifflin Harcourt, and other publishers. Wiley currently lives and writes in New York City.

## About the Artist

**Steve Cox** lives in Bath, England. He first designed toys and packaging for other people's characters. But he decided to create his own characters and turned full time to illustrating. When he is not drawing books he plays lead guitar in a rock band.

Publisher's Cataloging-In-Publication Data
Names: Blevins, Wiley. | Cox, Steve, 1961- illustrator. | Blevins, Wiley. Scary tales retold.
Title: The Bremen Town ghosts / by Wiley Blevins ; illustrated by Steve Cox.
Other Titles: Bremen town musicians. English.

Description: South Egremont, MA : Red Chair Press, [2017] | Interest age level: 006-009. |
    Summary: "Off to Bremen Town go Donkey, Cat, Dog, and Rooster. But music is not on their
    minds. They're tired of their cruel masters and set out in search of a better life. Is fate kind to
    the gang?"--Provided by publisher.

Identifiers: LCCN 2016934118 | ISBN 978-1-63440-165-4 (library hardcover) | ISBN 978-1-63440-
    169-2 (paperback) | ISBN 978-1-63440-173-9 (ebook)

Subjects: LCSH: Animals--Juvenile fiction. | Ghosts--Juvenile fiction. | Horror tales. | CYAC:
    Animals--Fiction. | Ghosts--Fiction. | LCGFT: Fairy tales.

Classification: LCC PZ7.B618652 Br 2017 (print) | LCC PZ7.B618652 (ebook) | DDC [E]--dc23

Scary Tales Retold first published by:
Red Chair Press LLC            PO Box 333            South Egremont, MA 01258-0333

Printed in the United States of America

0617 1P CGBF17

Some tales are old.
So old that the truth begins to rust.
What's the truth in this tale?
Only the ghosts can say.

Many years ago, an unlikely group of
animals became friends. They came from
homes where animals were not loved.

Donkey's owner kicked him when
he was slow. Beat him when he was fast.
And screamed at him all day.

Dog's owner was no kinder. He forced Dog to sleep in the mud. And he fed Dog only once a week.

Cat's owner was almost never home.
But when he was, he would push Cat
off his chair. And force him to sleep
on the cold roof.

Rooster's owner hated only one thing.
The morning crow of a rooster.
So every sunrise, he would throw
things at Rooster to stop him.

One day, each animal had had enough.
So when their owners left for the day,
each decided to run away.

"Hee-haw," said Donkey.
"To Bremen Town I will go."

"Ruff. Ruff. Grrr," said Dog.
"To Bremen Town I will go."

"Meow. Meow. Purr," said Cat.
"To Bremen Town I will go."

"Cock-a-doodle doo," said Rooster.
"To Bremen Town I will go."

On the road, the animals met.

They joined together and sang.

*Cock-a-doodle, meow,*
*Hee-haw, ruff.*
*Now we can escape*
*From a life too tough.*

Along their journey, the animal friends spotted a hut on a hilltop. "Maybe this will be a good place to live," said Donkey.

As they approached the hut, the animal
friends saw a light. A group of robbers
were inside counting their money and
feasting on a grand meal.

"We are so hungry," cried Rooster.
"How can we get some of that food?"
asked Donkey.
"Let's scare off the robbers," said Cat.
"We can pretend to be a ghost," said Dog.

So Dog climbed on top of Donkey. Cat climbed on top of Dog. And Rooster hopped on top of them all. They leaned against the window, casting a giant ghostly shadow. Then they began to make loud haunting noises.

Frightened, the robbers fled the hut.
And as they fled, the animals saw who the
robbers were. Their mean and evil owners!

The animal friends raced in. They munched
and crunched on the delicious feast.

Soon, they fell asleep.

From the bottom of the hill, the robbers watched.
"We have been tricked by our animals!" they said.
So they decided to take back the hut. But they
weren't the only ones who wanted the animals out.

The robbers tiptoed up the hill.
They surrounded the hut. Then on
the count of 1, 2, 3, they gave a
fearsome roar.

The animals dashed around the hut for a
place to hide. They tried one closet door.
Then another and another. But none would
open. Something was holding them shut.
And as the robbers burst in . . .

A gaggle of ghosts
floated into the room.

Plop! Flop! Drop!
In an instant the animals and
robbers fell dead from fright.

To this day their ghosts haunt the hut.
At night, visitors hear strange noises.
Screams of terrified animals. Moans of
trapped robbers. They are the last sounds
the visitors ever hear.

# THE END